'THE GARDEN GNOMES OF GRANTHAM MANOR'

G   1. PADDY PANTS DOWN

R   2. ARTHUR

A   3. GRUMPY MICK

N   4. ANDY'S SPACE ADVENTURE

T   5. LEG - A - LESS

H   6. HENRY'S NEAT & TIDY BUSH

A   7. LEAPING LEONARD

M   8. SEENO, HEARNO & SPEAKNO

~   9. THE WIZARD'S SLEEVE

M   10. GEOFF & DAVE'S SPORTING ANTICS

A   11. NANCY

N   12. THE NAUGHTY TRIPLETS

O   13. DARBY, TERRANCE & TRENT

R   14. THE THREE AMIGOS

Written by M F Katori 2020

Illustrated by M F Katori 2020

Wesley is a wizard,

he has a wizards sleeve.

He puts things right up in it,

and the gnomes all watch them leave.

They are in awe of Wesley

because he is so magic,

he puts a real good show on,

and is always so dramatic.

He took himself to Amsterdam

to learn a cool new trick.

It involved a ping-pong ball,
it really was quite slick.

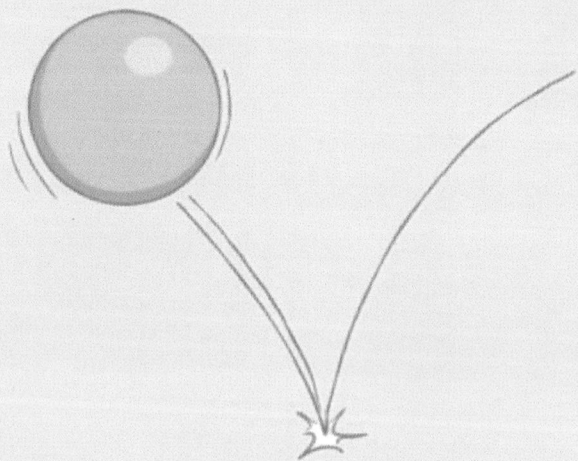

GRANTHAM MANOR

When Wesley mastered this illusion, he took himself off home.

To put his ping pong show on

for all the garden gnomes.

He put the ball into his sleeve,

it slipped right in it fit with ease.

He jumped up and down and
with a wiggle,
new this charade would be a
breeze.

The gnomes all watched with anticipation,

with abaited breath and expectation.

**Wesley did not fail to please,
as the ball shot out his other
sleeve.**

HOORAY

WOW

YIPPEE

WOW

OOO   WOW   GASP   WOW   OOO

He is so
amazing

WOW

He is so
fantastic

**The gnomes thought this
was quite fantastic.**

Wesley wanted to be

more dramatic.

He wondered if he could

fit more balls in...

Phew thirsty work

He worked on this until

his mouth went dry.

Which gave him a 'UREEKA' cry.

UREEKA!!

UREEKA!!

UREEKA

UREEKA

"All I need is lubrication to pull off this improved creation."

He greased his sleeve up

'til it was slippy.

Out all the balls shot, he shouted

YIPPEE!!

All the gnomes they cheered and cheered, they couldn't believe it when the balls appeared.

YAY WOOOO HIP HIP

HOORAY

ONE

TWO

THREE

FOUR

FIVE

SIX

SEVEN

EIGHT

NINE

TEN

and then

ELEVEN

THE GNOMES

ASKED???

"Then shoot them out so very quick,
they all shot out with ease."

Wesley replied:-

"A wizard never reveals his secrets,
I'm glad you enjoyed the show.

Don't think about it too long,
there are just some things you
shouldn't know!!"

If you like what you have read, then please leave a review.

That way I can keep on writing, lots and lots of books for you.

ALSO AVAILABLE

'THE BEAUTIFUL ISLAND OF POWLEY'

"A fantastically humorous nonsense adventure" for 2yrs and up.

Did you ever wonder what happened to the owl and the pussycat? Well I am here to tell you, so settle down and prepare to sail away on a magical journey to the place where the bong trees grow in this enchanting tale based on Edward Lear's "The owl and the pussycat."

Intrigued?

M F Katori's spellbinding and delightful tale of wit and charm will leave your little ones dreaming of the sights they would see if they went to "The Beautiful Island of Powley."

COMING SOON

OTHER TITLES IN THE GRANTHAM MANOR SERIES :

'THE PIXIES OF GRANTHAM MANOR'

'THE FAIRIES OF GRANTHAM MANOR'

'THE WITCHES OF GRANTHAM MANOR'

For more information about my books, short stories, news and events etc, please visit my website and sign up to my mailing list.

https://maxinekatori.wixsite.com/mfkatori

Many thanks

Printed in Great Britain
by Amazon